To
GRACYN

Your Grandma and
Grandpa Stache
♡ You!

2021

For Adela, Elaina, Faith and Zannah Rose. - MB

For my lovely niece Cee Cee. If I dreamed I had a daughter, that dream would be you! - JM

For Lauren, who I love and believe in... completely. - ML

Fifth Edition
2015

Scribble & Sons
2928 Cumberland Ave
Waco, Texas 76707
www.ScribbleAndSons.com

Baker, Margaret.
Ludy, Mark.
Matott, Justin.
When I Was A Girl... I Dreamed /
Written by Margaret Baker & Justin Matott/
Illustrations by Mark Ludy.
5th Ed.
p. cm.

Library of Congress Control Number: 2015949176

ISBN: 978-0-9916352-2-1

Printed in China

WHEN I WAS A
GIRL...
I DREAMED

WRITTEN BY MARGARET BAKER
& JUSTIN MATOTT

ILLUSTRATED BY MARK LUDY

Scribble&Sons
PUBLISHING

WACO, TEXAS

When I was a girl,

I dreamed great dreams

of who I'd be and where,

of places near and journeys far,

adventures wild and rare.

$\mathcal{I}$ dreamed I was the teacher,

of an eager, lively class.

I taught them reading, writing, math,

and prayed they all would pass.

$\mathcal{M}$any of my students

led extraordinary lives.

Imagine my joy when one naughty boy

received the Nobel Prize!

I dreamed I was a dancer,
so graceful, so refined.
Directors longed to sign me on,
and roles for me designed.

I jumped and twirled up on my toes.
I leapt and soared so high.
A princess in my pale pink shoes,
I felt like I could fly.

I dreamed I was an artist,
studied brushstrokes, mastered hues,
and painted on my canvas
the world's most splendid views.

My landscapes were in great demand.
The art world knew my name.
What a delight to know my work
had earned such lasting fame.

I dreamed I cared for animals,
for every kind of beast,
from the strong and mighty rhino
to the smallest and the least.

My patients came from far and wide,
from every stripe and nation.
I even cured the jungle king!
(I had quite a reputation).

I dreamed I built a robot
who could vacuum, cook and clean.
She even washed my windows!
What a marvelous machine.

She'd paint my nails and comb my hair,
then fix my supper, fast.
A fantastic friend, my robot maid,
we really had a blast!

I dreamed I was a diver
who explored the seas down deep.
I studied coral reefs and sea life
and exotic things that creep.

*S*uch an awesome mass of fish,
each one with its own style.
What a privilege to take close-ups
and to see that great white smile.

I dreamed I floated 'round the world
in a huge hot air balloon.
From L.A. to New York
on a sunny afternoon.

I saw mountains, valleys, cities, towns,
and oceans shore to shore.
All Seven Wonders of the World,
then discovered several more.

I dreamed I lived in Egypt,
seeking artifacts so rare.
I burrowed under pyramids
to see what might be there.

*A*nd what I found, you won't believe,
deep beneath the earth,
The Tomb of the Five Kings!
Of immense and untold worth.

I dreamed I had a clubhouse
that was stationed up in space.
I invited all my friends to come
to that exciting place.

We'd play volleyball and checkers,
talk at poolside, share a snack.
Though it was far, my rocket car
would zoom us there and back.

I dreamed I rode my faithful horse
out in the wild Wild West.
I rounded up the bandits,
and proved I was the best!

I hauled those villains into town
and restored the rule of law.
Was presented with the city's key.
The mayor was in awe.

I dreamed I was an athlete,
playing basketball for "State."
That season we won every game.
Our teamwork was first-rate.

*W*e made it to the finals,
all tied, the clock near zero.
I jumped, I aimed, I shot,
I SCORED! That night I was the hero.

I dreamed I owned a shopping mall,
and went on quite a spree.
I bought odds and ends for all my friends,
and even some for me.

Shoes and purses, jewelry, hats,
in boxes stacked so tall.
With a pair of dapper butlers
at our every beck and call.

I dreamed I was the President,
the leader of my land.
My goal was not to rule,
but rather seek to understand.

And so I listened closely,
read each postcard, every letter.
And together with all citizens,
we made our country better.

I dreamed that I wrote stories
of princesses and lords.
I even won a Newbery
and other book awards.

But the notes my readers sent to me
gave me far more pleasure.
To know that I'd inspired their hearts,
that is my greatest treasure.

Yes, as a girl I dreamed

great dreams.

Perhaps you dream them too.

Reach higher than the stars, my dears,

and your dreams...

will come true.

Written By:

Margaret Baker
is the mother of four girls and is married to the "man of her dreams." She loves kids, ice skating and reading children stories. She is a Princeton/Harvard graduate with a Ph.D in Chinese Literature. She has always dreamed of writing books for children and this is her first one. Margaret lives in Ann Arbor, Michigan.

Justin Matott
is the writer of many books including "When I Was A Boy... I Dreamed." He is a passionate soul who loves what he does and it shows. He is a regular speaker in schools and has the ability to communicate with kids in such a way that they "get it." Justin lives in Highlands Ranch, Colorado. Learn More @ JustinMatott.com.

Illustrated By:

Mark Ludy
is the author and illustrator of several books. His illustrative talent has recived praise from all over the world. With a style all his own he creatively reaches audiences every-where, be it through his Bic Pen or his hilarious sense of humor. Mark lives in Waco, Texas. Learn More @ MarkLudy.com.